The Bright Stars

Written by Monica Hughes

Illustrated by Julie Pla

Jess and Jack are members of the Bright Stars.

The coach picks Jess. It will be the
Bright Stars versus the Panthers.

The coach did not pick Jack.
Jack is fed up.

The coach tells Jack not to sulk.

It is kick-off!
Jess gets a shot at goal, but
she misses!

The Panthers get a shot at
goal, but they miss too.

The Bright Stars have a corner.
Jess is near the goal.

"Come on, Jess!" yells Jack.
Jess jumps and then ...

Jess is hurt!

"I can not get up," she moans.

Jess limps off.

Jack is little but he is quick.
He twists and turns.

He zigzags in and out of the
Panthers. They can not stop him.

Jack gets near the goal.
"Shoot!" yells Jess.
Jack shoots and ...

... it is a goal!
The Bright Stars win one-nil!

You are little but you are a big, bright star!

GRANNY FRANNY'S BIG ZOO RESCUE

Written and illustrated by
Sonia Beldom

For Tony

whose patience, illustration advice, sense of humour
and never-ending support has been my inspiration.

And for the precious little robin who visited every day
whilst writing this story.

A percentage of sales will be donated to the RSPB.

Jax and Ronni loved their Granny Franny's Zoosday Tuesdays.

There were always lots of animals to see and a perfect packed lunch with plenty of crunch.

It was the morning of the big zoo trip and Granny Franny was driving Jax and Ronni's class there on the big red bus.

She was up very early to make sure that everything was super sparkly and clean.

"Have I got time for a nice cup of tea, Thinkerbell?"
asked Granny Franny when she had finished.
Thinkerbell, the talking bus bell and Granny's best friend, had a think.

"SADLY NO, IT'S TIME TO GO.
IT'S A LONG WAY TO THE ZOO.
DON'T BE LATE FOR OUR SPECIAL DATE,
FOR THAT WILL NEVER DO."
she said with a loud DING DING.

The school children were very excited when Granny Franny arrived in her big red bus.

"Be careful getting on, make sure you have your packed lunches and have a wonderful day." said their teachers.

"Can you tell us a story, Thinkerbell?" asked Jax and Ronni when they set off. Thinkerbell was just starting the tale of Terry the Terrifying Tiger when there was a commotion from the top deck.

"LOOK! There's a giraffe in the park." shouted a very excited Mina.

"THEY'VE SEEN A GIRAFFE?
NOW DON'T MAKE ME LAUGH.
HOW COULD THAT BE?
IT WAS PROBABLY A TREE."
thought Thinkerbell.

Then she heard Ronni shout, "Wow!
Super cool! There are penguins
playing in the paddling pool!"

GR

Thinkerbell did what she did best and had a think.

"THIS CANNOT BE TRUE.
PENGUINS LIVE IN THE ZOO.
OR AT THE SOUTH POLE,
WHERE THEY'RE FOUND
ON THE WHOLE."

she pondered as she
pictured penguins in
their natural habitat.

"Now, can everybody calm down please?" asked
Granny Franny.

But the children didn't calm down one little bit.

"Check it out! Chimps are chasing around the churchyard."
chuckled Charlie.

"What an icy eyeful! There are polar bears right over there."
pointed Peter.

"Goodness gracious! That grazing goat is most audacious."
grinned Gregor who liked using very big words.

Granny Franny stopped the bus to see what all the fuss was about.

"I think I saw a lion lining up outside the butcher's shop." said Lea.

"Goosey goosebumps! I'm a bit scared of lions with their big pointy teeth and long sharp claws." said Granny Franny, hoping that Lea had imagined it.

Suddenly Thinkerbell's BUSNET buzzed with
an emergency message from Bugsy the bleeper on the jeep.

BLEEEEEP BLEEEEEP BLEEEEEP

"The zoo is in terrible trouble and we need your help.
Please come quickly." said the message.

Just as they turned right for the zoo, they saw a big sign that said ZOO CLOSED.

"Oh no!" cried the disappointed children.

"So the children were telling the truth." Granny Franny said to herself. She was now feeling a bit bad for not believing them. Meanwhile Thinkerbell and Bugsy were having a think about how to get the animals back.

"WE CAN GET THE PENGUINS ON THE BUS,
THE MONKEYS AND THE PIG,
BUT WHAT ABOUT THE ELEPHANTS?
I THINK THEY'RE FAR TOO BIG."

Within minutes they heard NEE-NAW, NEE-NAW, NEE-NAW as Saira Siren's ambulance came screeching around the corner, closely followed by Fifi Firebell's fire engine.

"Hello everybody. This looks like a big job so we've brought another friend with us." said Saira and Fifi.

The air filled with a very loud whirring noise as a big buzzy drone flew in.
"Hello everybody." boomed Spencer Speaker at full volume.
'Wow – flying around like that must be fun." said Granny Franny.
"Ha ha ha. It has its ups and downs." said Spencer.

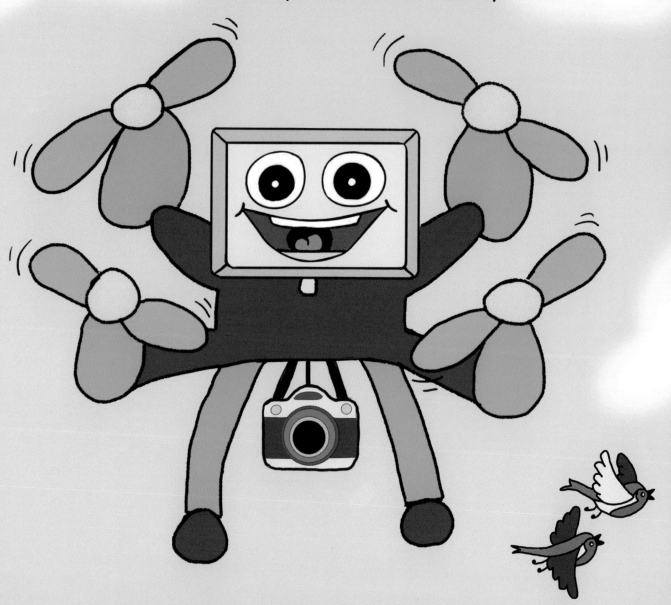

The children helped Thinkerbell draw a map to show where the animals were last spotted. Then with big bleeps, noisy nee-naws, clamorous clangs and deafening dings they set off on their big zoo rescue.

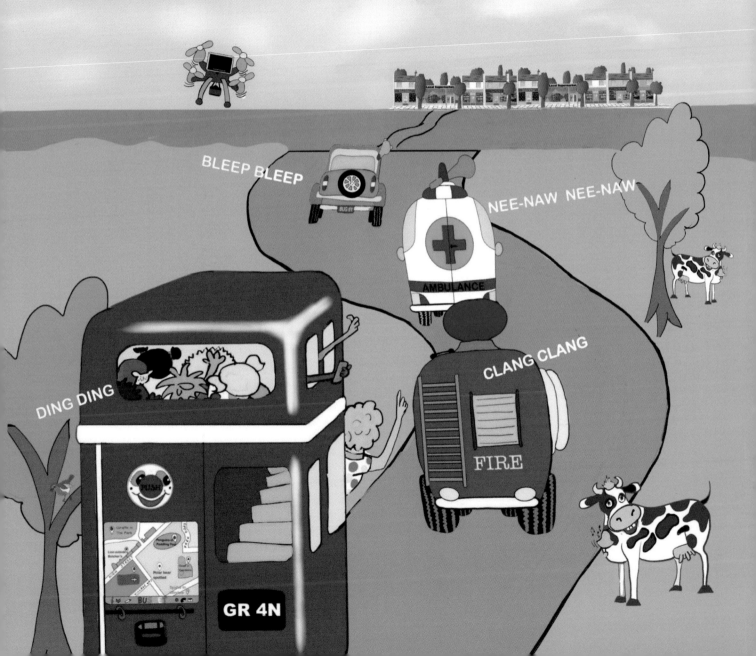

Granny Franny's first stop was the paddling pool.

"Oh dear. How am I going to stop the penguins from waddling off?" she sighed, scratching her head.

"I've got a tuna sandwich in my packed lunch." said Miko.
Thinkerbell was impressed with Miko's thinking.

"THAT'S AN EXCELLENT IDEA!
PENGUINS LOVE THEIR FISH.
I'M SURE THEY WILL BE TEMPTED
BY THIS FISHY-WISHY DISH."

It worked! The penguins came
waddling back and tucked in
to the tasty tuna.

Swan Lake
Deep water

Jax and Ronni had bananas in their lunchboxes. "Come and get them!" they shouted and the cheeky chimps bounced on board to enjoy their fabulous feast.

"Oh, trembling trifles! It's the big, scary lion next." groaned Granny Franny. Yes, even super brave grannies can be a teeny-weeny bit scared at times.

"I can help!" boomed Spencer. He flew off to pick up a selection of scrumptious sausages from Mr. Bones the butcher.

"Help!" whispered Granny Franny
as the big, scary lion got closer and closer.

She shut
her eyes
tight in fright
as he grabbed
all the sausages.
His favourites were
the veggie option as they
were super soft. Then Granny
Franny saw that he had no teeth
as he was a very old lion.

"What was I so scared of?" she chuckled
as the lion jumped on board the bus.

Granny Franny's big red bus was almost full of animals.

"ONLY TWO MORE ANIMALS TO GO.
THEY'RE HEAVY, BIG AND GREY.
WITH GREAT BIG BENDY CHUNKY TRUNKS,
AND JUST A MILE AWAY."

said Thinkerbell, as they drove up the hill.

At the top of the hill were the two enormous elephants.

The twins made a big splashy fountain for the elephants to play in while Granny Franny slipped harnesses around their necks so that they could safely be led back to the zoo.

They were nearly back to the zoo when there was a deafening

FFFFFFSSSSSSSSHHHHHHH

"Oh wonky wheel nuts! I've got a flat tyre." sighed Granny Franny
as she plonked her shiny shoe into yucky, mucky elephant poo.

Everybody helped. Jax and Ronni sprayed and swept the road while Lydia and Miko helped Granny change her wheel.

At last they were ready to go and Granny's shoe was all sparkly and clean again.

Ziggy the zookeeper was very happy to see the animals back safely.

"Thank you everybody. You've all been amazing." he said to the children and gave each one a special souvenir, a free family ticket and food to feed their favourite animals.

"And this is for you." said Ziggy, as he surprised a very thirsty Granny Franny with a super special afternoon tea.

Everybody agreed that it was the best Zoosday Tuesday ever.

Printed in Poland
by Amazon Fulfillment
Poland Sp. z o.o., Wrocław

65092671R00021